My MOM and ME

by **Alyssa Satin Capucilli** • illustrated by **Susan Mitchell**

LITTLE SIMON

New York   London   Toronto   Sydney

When it's only my mom and me . . .

and have long
picnic talks.

we take crunchy
leaf walks,

When it's only my *mami* and me . . .

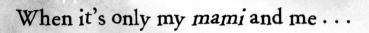

Mami means "mom" in Spanish.

When it's only
my *ima* and me . . .

Ima means "mom" in Hebrew.

and share frosty nose hugs.

we sip cocoa in mugs,

we let our kites fly,

and watch clouds dancing by.

When it's only my *màmà* and me . . .

Màmà means
"mom" in Mandarin.

We run barefoot and cheer,
"Summer's here, summer's here!"
When it's only my *màmà* and me.

and also each night.

we celebrate every day,